ISIS

ISIS

DOUGLAS CLEGG

Illustrations by
Glenn Chadbourne

Vanguard Press
A Member of the Perseus Books Group

First special, limited hardcover edition published in 2006 by Cemetery Dance
Publications. This hardcover edition published in 2009 by Vanguard Press, a
member of the Perseus Books Group.

Designed by Pauline Brown
Set in 12.5 point Garamond

Library of Congress Cataloging-in-Publication Data

Clegg, Douglas, 1958–
Isis / Douglas Clegg.
   p. cm.
  ISBN 978-1-59315-540-7 (alk. paper)
  1. Haunted houses—England—Fiction. 2. Death—Fiction. 3. Brothers
and sisters—Fiction. 4. Grief—Fiction. I. Title.
PS3553.L3918I75 2009
813'.54—dc22
                                   2009009776

Vanguard Press books are available at special discounts for bulk purchases in
the U.S. by corporations, institutions, and other organizations. For more in-
formation, please contact the Special Markets Department at the Perseus
Books Group, 2300 Chestnut Street, Suite 200, Philadelphia, PA 19103, or
call (800) 810-4145, ext. 5000, or e-mail special.markets@perseusbooks.com.

10 9 8 7 6 5 4 3 2 1

For
Mindy

ACKNOWLEDGMENTS

With thanks to Raul Silva, M. J. Rose, Glenn Chadbourne, Simon Lipskar, Francine LaSala, Roger Cooper, Amanda Ferber, Georgina Levitt, and all of Vanguard Press.

FOR READERS

Be sure to go to www.DouglasClegg.com for the free, private newsletter and get instant access to exclusive extras and treats, including novels, novellas, stories, screensavers, and more.

Part One

The Window

Jack, swing up, and Jack swing down
Up to the window, over the ground.
Swing over the field and the garden wall—
But watch out for Jack Hackaway if you should fall.

—*Nursery rhyme, 1800s*

ONE

❧ 1 ❧

"Beware a field hedged with stones," our gardener, Old Marsh, told me in his smoky voice with its Cornish inflections, as he pointed to the land near the cliff. "See there? The hedge holds in. Will not let out. Things lurk about places like that. Unseen things."

A house, I suppose, is a stone-hedged field.

A tomb, as well.

The place where the stone-hedges ended, as they grew round our house and the gardens, was an old cave entrance that had been turned into a mausoleum beneath the ground, carved out for centuries for the bones of my ancestors.

❧ 2 ❧

The locals called it the Tombs, although it was much more than merely a series of subterranean burial chambers.

It had been carved from rock by the local miners for some early Villiers ancestor and had been used just two years before my birth, when my grandmother had died. Her coffin was sealed up in granite and plaster within the Tombs, and there were spaces for other Villiers to come. My mother made me swear that I would never allow her to be buried there. "I don't like that place," she told me. "It's cold and horrible and primitive. Put me in a churchyard with a proper marker. Do you promise me?" Certain that her death was years away, I promised her whatever she asked. I coaxed a smile from her when I demanded that upon my own death, she have the ragman cart me away to the rubbish pile.

What lay below the Tombs had once been a sacred site to the Cornish people, more than a thousand years earlier. It had been a cave, leading down the cliff-side through a series of narrow passages out to sea. It was believed to be an entrance to the Otherworld—the Isle of Apples, it was sometimes called—where a stag-god and a crescent-moon mother goddess ruled.

There had been a legend, once, of a Maiden of Sorrow, who had traveled deep in the earth to the Isle of Apples to find her lover who had died a terrible death in a distant battle. When she had returned, she brought him with her and held his hand as they emerged from the winding caves into the sunlight. But when others saw the couple, they cried out in terror—for her lover's eyes were black as pitch, and he had no mouth upon his face, just a seal of flesh as if he had not formed completely upon his journey back to the land of the living. The villagers knew he was not meant to be among them, yet the Maiden would not allow him to return to the earth. The legend went that the Maiden lived with him there at the edge of the sea, but he could not speak, nor did his eyes return to life, nor could anyone look him in the eye, lest they be driven mad from seeing the Otherworld reflected in his glance.

When someone in the nearby village was near death, the Maiden's lover would appear at their doorway and seek entrance, as if trying to find his way back to his soul, which had remained on the other side.

There was also a large round granite stone in the field at the edge of the sunken garden, not ten paces from the Tombs. Called the Laughing Maiden, it was believed that once in early times of the Christians, another maiden went out and laughed at the priest on Sabbath day and was turned to stone there.

I went to this stone as a girl with our gardener, who believed all the old tales. Old Marsh was thought of as the local color—the crackpot old-wives-tale man of the earth who believed all the old stories and would walk backward around a graveyard to avoid upsetting the dead. He had been known to plant sheep-nettle at the stables when one of the horses had gotten sick, "to keep out bewitchments," he'd say quite proudly. He knew a story for every stone, every fountain, every plant, and every tree at Belerion Hall. Old Marsh took it all seriously, and he warned me against upsetting spirits by changing the old gardens too much. "They like their flowers as they like them," he said when I had been uprooting the weed-like milk thistle. "Bad luck to do that, for the saying goes, 'Set free the thistle and hear the devil whistle.'"

At the Tombs, he gave me the most serious advice. "Never go in, miss. Never say a prayer at its door. If you are angry, do not seek revenge by the Laughing Maiden stone, or at the threshold of the Tombs. There be those who listen for oaths and vows, and them that takes it quite to heart. What may be said in innocence and ire becomes flesh and blood should it be uttered in such places."

ISIS

I looked upon the rock chamber with its small double doorways and its chains and lock, a ruins more than a mausoleum, sunken into the grassy earth with a view of the wide gray sea beyond it, and remembered such stories.

I did not intend ever to cross its threshold.

TWO

❧ 1 ❧

I was born Iris Catherine Villiers, and in the days before we came to Belerion Hall, my parents were still in love with each other. My older brothers—the "twin Villiers" as old Mrs. Haworth would later call them—Spencer and Harvard, and my eldest brother, Lewis (whom I rarely saw once we had left our first home), made up the children. To tell them apart, Spence parted his hair on the left, and Harvey, on the right. Harvey had a birthmark behind his ear, while Spence had none. Spence smelled, in the summer, distinctly of dirt and pond water, while Harvey had a fragrance as if he'd rolled in lavender.

I could tell them apart from the moment my memories began—for Harvey had always been pure warmth and gentleness whereas Spence was casually cruel and often cold, though perfectly nice in his own way. At my birth, Lewis was six, and Harvey and Spence were three.

I did not have a moment in my life when one of them did not occupy my time in some way, whether for good or ill. Of the three, Harvey loved me from the moment I could remember. I loved him in the sisterly fashion for he was my protector in many ways from the rough-and-tumble of other children, and from his own twin, who resented the new baby in the family.

My earliest memories were of delight and love. We had a happy, bright, and beautiful mother who hailed from Chicago and had been, briefly, an actress and then a pianist. She had married my father, a British citizen, when they ran into each other outside of the Carthage Club in Manhattan before lunch. They fell in love over soup and roast beef at the Bellamy on Fifth Avenue, spoke of the future after cocktails at the "26," and were married before City Hall had closed, much to the chagrin of my mother's parents. My mother never again played the piano, and her only acting would be later, in local amateur theatricals that often thrilled me, for they seemed to be made of magic and stardust.

I was born in the summer cottage at Fisher's Island that my American grandparents had given my parents as a wedding gift. I grew up an island girl, rarely ever going to the mainland, for I had a tutor and nanny at our house. I walked barefoot nearly all the summer, though my father called my mother "primitive" for allowing her children such immodesty.

My brothers took up slingshots when I was five. Harvey, as a joke, aimed at a bird in a tree, but when he'd shot it, he felt terrible that the bird had been hit and fell to the earth. We both ran to it, and Harvey lifted it into his hands and kissed it. He let it go and it flew off. "It was only stunned," he said, and I told him, "Promise me never to do that again." He promised. I made him promise a second time. We watched the bird fly off across the pink summer twilight, and then we went to bury his slingshot forever.

My brothers parted for their boarding school during the week and then returned Friday evenings to spend the weekends on the island. We played all the games of childhood, and when I was afraid to go on the swing that hung from the oak tree in our yard, Harvey had told me, "But we're the Great Villiers Brother-and-Sister Trapeze Act!"

He would beat his chest and call out, "The greatest circus on the island! Come one, come all, to the Great

Villiers Trapeze Brother-and-Sister Act!" And then he'd swing me up in his arms and rock me as if I were in a cradle. Gingerly, he would step onto the low swing, holding onto me with one hand while he squatted down upon the plank. We would swing up and down for hours, and he never once dropped me or let me go.

As we both became more comfortable with the Great Villiers Trapeze Brother-and-Sister Act, he'd swing me around and when I grew scared again, he'd say, "Close your eyes and count to ten, and when you open them, you'll be on the ground." And so we began to do minor acrobatics, which scared my mother half to death, for he might stand on the swing and lift me up to his shoulders while we flew out over the grass. I smelled summer lavender upon him, and sometimes I smelled the sea, too, for it was just in sight. I had no other friends on the island, and my other brothers paid no attention to me.

Harvey taught me the nursery rhymes our father had taught him when he had been my age, including the swinging rhyme about Jack Hackaway. "Jack Hackaway is a little troll who takes children to the goblins when they fall," he said, and now and then to scare me a little he might say, as we swung, "Who goes there? Jack Hackaway, is that *you*?"

Sometimes I felt as if I were flying with wings on when we swung together. He always treated me as if I were the special one in the family. I loved those memories, and I cherish them even now.

By my seventh year, my father had been called to Burma by the British government, for there was a war and he was a trader in wars. So many wars came and went while I was a child that even in later years, I barely remembered what my father looked like, or how he spoke, for it was like remembering a haunting stranger seen once in a crowded train station and then never again.

My mother and my older brothers and I were packed off to my father's ancestral home across the sea to watch over his own father, who was close to death. We moved into Belerion Hall, traveling from my beloved cottage off the Long Island Sound to the rocky cliffs of the furthest perch of Cornwall.

My first sight of the place was painful. I saw in its slate-gray curtain of rain nothing but a large prison, so unlike the delicate, wispy cottage I considered our true home, with its azalea and rhododendron bushes all around and the honeysuckle in midsummer. This new home had dead gardens that brimmed with the skeletons of briars, while moss slickened its rusty stones. Belerion Hall seemed like a millwork factory that had closed years ago, a great turgid red brick monolith to an unhappy era.

If Belerion Hall had the puritanical face of a factory, then my grandfather could best be described as the Gray Minister, which is what my brother Harvey named him immediately after our first encounter. "The Gray Minister lurks," he'd whisper to me as I giggled. "He listens at keyholes." Or after supper, when we played charades in the nursery, Harvey would make a signal in the air with his hands as if waving and say, "The Gray Minister comes a-tap-tapping." This got the both of us in trouble when Spence told our grandfather of the nickname, and the elderly man came at Harvey with his gold-tipped cane, leaving my brother with bloodied trousers. Harvey had protected me, pushing me behind one of the many curtained alcoves of the corridors so that I might not be found for punishment.

Our grandfather was a tall, gaunt man of seventy, with a white wisp of beard like a goat, and a long pale face that rose up to meet the bits of peppery scrub hair left him upon his scalp.

He had eyes that always seemed red and smudged with sleeplessness, and his lips were thin and drawn back over an uneven row of teeth. He seemed perpetually smeared with a slight layer of coal dust, as if he'd been rooting around in the cellars. He rarely wore anything other than a gray coat, and beneath this, a stiff white shirt with a heavy white collar, both of which the maid had to press daily. His shoes and trousers were gray, as well, and he carried the Bible with him, though it was worn and its binding crackled and threatened to turn to dust each time he opened it.

"To spill thy seed," he often warned Spence and Harvey, "is to invoke the wrath of God."

To me, he would say (even when I was eleven or twelve), "Woman, thou art a temptation to Man. Clean thyself and thy thoughts. Scrub the unholy places of thy body, and bind thy flesh that it may be secret from our eyes."

His mania did not limit itself to us. He waggled his finger at my mother, declaiming verse and psalm and invoking the deity as if the Lord were his personal servant. My mother had enough, and by the end of our first year at Belerion Hall, she locked her father-in-law into the North Wing of the estate. While servants might go there to care for him, we children could only see him on Christmas and on his birthday.

Still, we heard his shouts of wrath and brimstone and Babylon from the windows of the North Wing, often late into the night. The Gray Minister stood there in the smear of light from the flickering lamp at the window and cried out ungodly things upon our heads or upon the heads of the kings of the world.

"When your father returns," my mother told me as she tucked me in one night when I had been agitated over my grandfather's caterwauling, "we will find your grandfather a proper place. He is not himself. His memories are gone. This ceaseless rain must also prey upon him. We must pity him." She kissed me on the forehead, and we said our prayers together as my grandfather continued crying out at the top of his lungs from the windows of the North Wing, "The Whore of Babylon rides upon the King of Hell! I have seen her! I have seen her! The Great Harlot! The Devil's Dam!"

I loathed the place in the rainy times. My mother had a peculiar ailment that seemed part sorrow and part silence and grew worse when the weather grew rough and cold. In the winters, she took to her bed for weeks

at a time, only seen by a nurse and the girl who took her supper. My mother's headaches increased then, and she had begun getting deliveries in the afternoon from a druggist in the village whose boy dropped off two packages of tincture of laudanum, three times a week; and if the boy on the bicycle did not come, Mrs. Haworth sent Percy, our gardener's son, into the village for a small bottle of *Dr. Witherspoon's Vita-Health Tonic*, which smelled distinctly of rum.

Once or twice I slipped in to see her while she ate, and she would stare off at the ceiling and run her fingers through my hair and talk aimlessly.

"Your father is important, you know that. He must be away. He must be. But it is hard sometimes. We all miss him," she said with a faint smell of tonic on her breath. "Your hair is pretty. It seems golden. In the summer, we can go to London. Wouldn't that be fun? Yes, it would be. Perhaps your father will meet us there. We can go to the theater or to the shops and have high tea, if you like. We can hire a driver. Or the train. Perhaps the train."

I did not see her much during the stormy days, for it saddened me more than the mad cries of my grandfather at the upper windows.

❧ 2 ❧

When the sun came out—for the summers at Belerion Hall were often long and pleasant—I saw the distant stone arches out along the tidal island that seemed to float atop turquoise waves. I could sit near the cliff's edge on a beautiful summer's day and imagine the white sand below the cliffs to be full of pirate treasure. My first governess told me of the seven stones in the old harbor to the west called "The Tin Men"; they had once been miners and had gone so deep into the earth that they were turned to rock itself. Now they sat in the sea, having swallowed enemy ships that had attacked the port centuries before. I loved the legends and tales, and in the village, where some of the folk spoke the old language, I began to learn a bit of it slowly and loved being able to say a word or two in Cornish.

During the long stretches of summer, my mother felt better and seemed cured of her malady—at least for a handful of months. No boy rode a bicycle in with a package of laudanum, and no empty bottles of *Dr. Witherspoon's* stood along the edge of her bedside table. We would go to London on weekend trips and stay at fine hotels and see plays or wander art museums and eat creamy cakes and tarts at tea. I expected to see our father on these trips, but he did not return from his war business, though we received telegrams and letters from him constantly.

On bright days, our mother would take us into the village. While my brothers wandered the streets, poking their heads in and out of shops and meeting the local boys and girls, I would go with my mother to her Ladies' Club, where, in late July and August, the charity theatricals were organized, much to my delight. These mostly were for children, and they were required to be educational as well as entertaining, so my mother managed to steer the ladies toward Greek and Egyptian myth and drama, for she had played Medea and Persephone in her own youth and knew many of these dramas. The summer I was twelve, we did the *Tragic Tale of Isis and Osiris*, written by a Mrs. Wilfred Jasper of London. It was a mercifully brief series of skits with very little dialogue, as part of a local theatrical fundraiser for the Wayward Girls Sea Cottage that the nuns of Saint Pedrog's ran.

My brother Harvey played Osiris, Spence played Set, and I was Isis. "I don't understand," Harvey said, when he read the play over. "Why does Isis keep having to do this?"

"What?" I asked. "She seems wonderful to me."

"That's because you're playing her," he said. "But if Osiris is dead, why doesn't she just let him be?"

"Yes!" Spence laughed, clapping his hands. "Let him just be dead."

I felt my face grow warm from a kind of sadness, for I took the play and my character of Isis very seriously. "Because she loves him. She doesn't want him dead."

"Rubbish. She's just being obstinate," Spence said, with a big smile on his face as if he were talking about me instead of Isis herself.

My mother played the goddess Nut, who also was the storyteller of the playlet. Others from the village and the local shops played parts in this and other short plays based on classical themes, and most of the village turned out for the event. The girl backstage painted my face so that I looked exotic and fairly wicked.

We didn't have an Egyptian headdress, so, instead, a crown was made of tinfoil and paper. I felt as if I had turned into a woman when I put it on my head. As Isis, I might have been the star of the show, but Spence, as Set, hammed it up and got all the applause. The twins were sixteen at the time, and not terribly happy to be forced into the Ladies' Club charity show, but once they saw pretty girls in the audience, they perked up.

Harvey, poor Osiris, didn't like the part where he climbed into the trunk at the banquet. He told me before the play began that it scared him to be in such a small space, particularly with Spence shutting it up and laughing like a devil when he closed him in. During rehearsals, Harvey nearly shivered when he looked down at the trunk, and my mother had to pull him aside and speak softly to him in order to get him to lie down in it. "You'll only be in it for a moment or two," she told him. "It will remain unlocked. I promise I will make sure."

He had glanced over at me and whispered, "Sometimes being scared is silly. I'm too old for it, aren't I?"

And I called him "Silly" and told him that there was nothing to be afraid of in a box.

I had an idea to help him overcome his fear. I drew him close to me. I whispered in his ear, behind which his birthmark lurked, and told him, "Don't be afraid. When you get in, close your eyes and count to ten. By the time you open them, you can get out of the box."

He grinned, and messed up my hair with his hand. "Sometimes you're smarter than me, and that's when I worry."

He kissed me at the edge of the lips, and I felt warmth on my face from that kiss through the whole play.

He played his part gamely and was given a standing ovation when Isis brought him back to life after Set had strewn pieces of him all along the Nile. The children who played the crocodiles were adorable, and they wagged their cornhusk tails to much hilarity.

My mother's performance dazzled me. She had a stage presence like none of the other ladies of that group. I imagine now that she would have been a great actress if she had not met my father, for she seemed more alive on stage than she ever did beyond it. I saw her as more than merely my mother when she made her first appearance and gave a speech about King Ra refusing to allow her to have children. Wrapped in a winding sheet made to re-semble a tunic, her heavy breasts nearly visible through the thin cloth, she looked as if she were a heroine stepped out of a Delacroix, an alternate "Liberty Leading Her People."

My mother became the essence of summer for me, for that was when she was with us the most. We planted

wisteria for me along the walkway and terraces, and more lavender for Harvey to use in his bath. He in turn helped Old Marsh and his son as they planted rows of new flowers and brought old bulbs back to life late in the season. Harvey would be covered in mud and dirt, and he'd wave to me as he followed the others into the Thunderbox Room, the water closet and sink area where the workmen washed up.

Harvey told me later that he preferred their company to Spence's and "the other snobs' at school." The kitchen girl adored him and made him special treats and gifts of soaps and candles. I was nearly jealous of her as she tried to enchant Harvey and steal him from us. I asked him about her once, and he grinned as if he understood my fears. "Oh, she's a nice girl, and works hard, but there's a boy in the village who has been in love with her since they both were children. She'll marry him and move above his shop someday, I think. But she is sweet, isn't she?"

He always ended up with me, and we gardened and walked, and I taught him to paint landscapes out by the cliff's edge. We planted our favorite flowers along the outer edge of the stone-hedged gardens, and more wisteria, and a funny little local flower called Sea-Star-Cross for Lewis, who, on his infrequent trips back from university for a few summer days, enjoyed the blue-white color of it. "And for Spence," Harvey might joke as he dug a trowel into the earth for planting, spattering up some dirt at me, "A bit of dirt!"

Harvey and I began planting mint and that small herb called "sirus-hen," with its fragrant and tangy odor, and we had a glorious summer or two. Mother cleaned out the dead brush of the garden and threw it over the cliff's edge as if to banish it from our land. We all worked together with Old Marsh and Percy to bring back the sunken gardens along the low hillside until, finally, when the blossoms came and the sun overwhelmed the sky, I found reason enough to love the house and grounds.

✎ 3 ✎

Somewhere during those summers, I could block my grandfather's stern and irrational lectures of God and the devil so that even on the stormiest days (for we had more of these than sunny ones) I explored Belerion Hall and the cliffside as if it were my own private doorway into wonderland itself.

Old Marsh had been trimming the overgrowth around the garden and saw my brother and me wandering toward the Tombs. He came out and sat with us for a bit, lighting his yellowed pipe, and told us about their legends. "Many bones are there. I seen 'em. In a pile, in stone coffins, some, but mostly just out in piles. Not a good place to play for a child like you, and you, Master Harvey, ought to know better."

"Are you chastising me, sir?" Harvey said, a mischievous grin upon his face.

"I would not do such a thing, sir, but these places are old and rotted. Your grandmother meant to seal it up before . . . well, before she passed. But here it remains."

"I'm too old to be frightened by such fairy tales," I said. "I know about the Maiden of Sorrow and her lover."

"Have you heard about the boy who brought back the dead warriors?" Old Marsh puffed on his pipe, and I could nearly see a little boy in the smoke that came from it.

I smiled at him. "A boy did that?"

"Back in those times when the Villiers were dukes and duchesses. See those rocks?"

"The Tin Men," I said, knowing this legend.

"When the enemies came, sometimes they got past 'em. Sometimes they killed everyone here. But one boy lived. He put the bones inside the Tombs here and he decided to pray to the old gods of the heathens so that magic could happen. He went first to the Laughing Maiden and called up spirits, and then in the Tombs, to bring the bones to life. And he raised warriors from the times of the Romans, and they came out—all made of bones and dirt. But they raised their swords and spears and they defeated the invaders. And that boy. That boy . . .”

“Summoned them?” I asked. “How?”

“Oh, I shouldn’t tell you, miss. Summoning’s a terrible business. Ancient words and spells, terrible things,” Old Marsh said, his hacking cough taking him over for a moment and making me think he might fall over from the force of it. “I dread even speaking of it, miss. It’s never the dead you bring back. It’s the soul of death itself, in the bodies of the dead. The Maiden of Sorrow learned that true enough, too. This boy learned it, the hard way. He was vengeful, this child.”

“Was he a Villiers?” Harvey asked.

“Perhaps,” Marsh said. “But he hadn’t learned how to make the dead . . . die again. He only knew how to raise the dead, learned from an old witch from out on the moors. To send them back to the Isle of Apples,

where all warriors live like kings, the dead made him promise to give them his first-born child when the boy grew up and took a wife. If he did not, they told him, they would come and drag him and his bride into the earth with them, where they would live between the living and the dead until the last of the world was finished."

"And did he give them his first born?" I asked, a bit fearful of the answer.

"Of course he didn't. Would you? He forgot about his vow. A boy he were, and none too bright. When he became a man, he married a lovely girl from Bodmir Moor. They had their first child the Christmas after they married. Only when he began to hear the scratching at the windows did he remember his promise. He went to priests for removal of this curse, but none could help. But you understand, the trick of calling up the dead is a one-way street, miss. For no one—no priest, no king, no saint—knows how to send the dead back where they came from. When the dead have been promised, the dead must be paid.

"No, he did not want to give up his child. Who would? He ran to the ends of the earth with his wife and son. He did not think the bones of the Tombs here at

Belerion Hall would find him across a sea. But the dead, they find paths—highways—what no living soul knows unless they been to the other side. These paths go beneath the earth, beneath the ocean itself.

"Though I weren't there, nor anyone I know, I heard—one day—when a local peddler went 'round to sell wares, he saw black marks as if fire scorched the house, yet nothing burned. And their shoes and slippers remained where they had stood before they were dragged off. The only signs that they'd had a child— a boy of seven by then—were some wooden toys off in a corner and a child's finger, severed at the second knuckle when he had been pulled into that between-place by the warriors. Written upon the walls of the house, in the ancient language of the dead, were the words 'Come Ye Not Here to Sleep or Slumber.'" Here, Marsh stopped and glanced over at me to see if I believed the story. "And you know what they found the very next day, miss?"

"What?" I asked, my heart nearly leaping to my throat.

He pointed to the doors of the Tombs. "Those very doors. Open, where they had been locked. Three bodies at the threshold."

"*It was them,*" I whispered.

He nodded. "Their fingers," he rubbed the tips of his fingers together as he said this, "and the soles of their feet. All blackened. As if they'd been burned. The little son, the third finger of his right hand, cut off at the second knuckle. Upon their foreheads, ancient markings. Heathen symbols. It were that boy, grown up. His bride. And his son. Their spirits live between worlds, for a promise broken is a newborn curse. Death has a price, and all who bargain with the dead must pay it. You must never sleep there, for the dead enter your dreams. They look for ways back to this world. See that?"

He pointed around Belerion Hall's property to the stone wall that surrounded the gardens and the Tombs and ran along the edge of the cliffs by the Laughing Maiden rock. "Beware a field hedged with stones. See there? The hedge holds in. Will not let out. Things lurk about places like that. Unseen things. In the garden, in the Tombs, up along the flagstone walk beneath the windows, even down in the Thunderbox Room, for the cellars are stone-hedges, too." He chuckled at this last admission. "Even in places in a stone foundation. It's all held in by those stones, which were put in place after those three bodies were found at the doorway of the Tombs."

"To hold that boy and his bride and his son here forever?" I asked.

He shook his head. "Not them, though it might have done. No, it was so that if any should ever again call up such dead in times of trouble, the dead could not find their ways out to the highways to hunt down the ones who had summoned them. The stone-hedges blind and confuse them and keep them from knowing the paths that the dead would know."

"I wish I could see the dead," I said, too brightly.

"The old people had a way of doing it," Old Marsh said, but he pointed his pipe at me as if about to scold me. "You mustn't, miss. But there is a game children play sometimes that comes from the old days. They take a blindfold and spin around, and them's what's got the touch, they talk with the dead."

"Blindman's buff?" I clapped my hands together. "Lovely! We shall play it and call the dead."

"No, miss," the gardener said, "never do that. The dead must sleep, and we must leave them be. Only God's meant to wake 'em, on Doomsday. Not for us to do it."

As Harvey walked with me back to our home, he nudged me and said in a bad approximation of Old

Marsh's Cornish accent, "Beware a field hedged with stones, deary, for unseen dead look for their paths but canna git out."

"But Old Marsh believes it."

"Yes, he does," Harvey chuckled. "He plants his corn by the dark of the moon, and he won't let a black dog set foot in the gardens. I heard he pays one of the old women in town to keep the Evil Eye off him, as well. He is quite the nutter. But, miss," again he imitated Old Marsh's voice, growling a bit as he spoke, "don't be entering the Tombs on Lammas night 'less ye have bathed in holy water and said yer prayers. Ye must nev'r sleep there for the dead enter yer dreams, miss."

I ignored all warnings one afternoon when I stole the keys to the Tombs from the little desk that Mrs. Haworth kept for her accounts and papers—and crouched down to open its door.

THREE

❧ 1 ❧

I did not go far in my exploration, but stood just inside the low door and looked down upon a kind of rock shelter.

It smelled of mold and earth. Though I had no candle, I could see the stone tombs as well as what seemed to be a pile of rubbish—carriage wheels and thin wooden boards, no doubt thrown into the Tombs within the past sixty years by my grandfather.

I thought of the boy and the warriors.

The story of the Maiden of Sorrow and her undead lover.

The Laughing Maiden who had been turned to stone by God.

I stepped back into daylight and crouched down, locking the doors, for I felt as if I had intruded on something holy by looking into the place of the dead.

❧ 2 ❦

In summer, I had no fear of the Tombs.

In winter, I grew sad watching it from the upstairs windows, for it made me think of death, as did the storms and my mother's sorrows.

On rainy days, I explored my grandfather's immense and musty library, with its volumes of strange and wonderful books. It had no windows at all, so I could forget the gray wintry world outside. Its ceiling looked like elegant chocolates from a London confectionery, and it had bookcases so high that I had to climb ladders to see it all. I crept over to the hearth rug with several books and lay there in front of the huge stone fireplace to begin my escape from Belerion Hall through the pages of novels and histories.

❧ 3 ❦

I worked my way through the Latin texts and through many of the classics that I could find. Other treasures were also buried here, including love letters my grandfather wrote my grandmother when they were both young, and drawings that my father had made as a boy in the margins of primers that had been saved.

My grandfather had kept a small pile of nude photographs of women, tucked behind an oversized 1835 edition of the Bible with a dark snakeskin cover. I sifted through these pictures, marveling at this secret wickedness of the Gray Minister. I looked upon these figures as if they would teach me what being a woman was within the world of men. I made up names for each of the girls—Biblical names like Delilah and Rahab and Ruth and Naomi and Jezebel, of course. I did not see them as lascivious in the least, for they seemed as my mother and I had in our pageant—works of art posed by a photographer who gave them flowers in their hair, or a tasteful hand drawn over their private parts.

Even Jezebel, the naughtiest of them, had a garland of daisies across her small belly, and though her head was cocked back slightly and her legs parted, she seemed to be contemplating eternity as she lay there. I knew this was a gentlemen's collection, but there was something pristine about these women, who, as nudes, could have been statues in great museums.

I located the page in the Bible where each woman was mentioned and pressed the corresponding picture of the nude into that page. I drew Harvey to the library to show him the pictures. He acted shocked at seeing them, and told me they were not meant for delicate young ladies. But I showed him Rahab and Delilah and asked him, "Do you think she is lovely?"

He blushed and shook his head. "No, not at all. Not lovely at all. Put those away, Iris. We really should burn them."

As I wandered deeper into my grandfather's library— for behind every book was another, and behind every bookcase, another could be drawn out if the latch were located—I also found books of a very different nature.

My grandfather's old library still contained his books on the occult, for though he beat the Good Book with one fist, he studied demonology in order to learn the names of the devils he wished to cast out of the world. I spent many hours, unnoticed by even my governess, in the old mahogany-lined library and delighted in the wicked books. I read grimoires and the medieval texts as I learned Latin in the morning and the tales of witch-finders and demon-raisers before tea.

I shared this with Harvey, who was—at first—aghast at my grandfather's extensive occult collection, but soon joined me in delight as we began writing secret notes to each other, left around the house, in some ancient coded language supposedly created by the Chaldean Demon-Raisers or the *Medieval Witch Alphabet*. Harvey left little jokes for me that I then had to translate from the strange symbols of the codes, and I left brief notes of "Spence on warpath" or "The Gray Minister knows your sins" under his tea saucer, or folded neatly into one of his favorite magazines.

❧ 4 ❧

One night, after supper, I began crying for no reason that I knew. Harvey took me for a walk along the stone-hedges of the sunken gardens by the full moon's light. The air was heavy and smothering with spring fragrances, and damp with recent rain. "Why so sad?" he asked.

Although many things had been bothering me, I ended up speaking of our mother and her sorrows. Finally, I said, "And it's because of our father."

"Ah," Harvey said.

"It's as if . . . as if . . ." I fought back tears. "As if he's dead."

"But he's not."

"No. He's in India or Burma or Australia or Africa. Everywhere but here."

"He is important for this country."

"But not us."

"No, not us," he said, kissing the top of my head. "I know. I know. Let's summon the dead, Iris. They can go bring father to us." He chuckled, and I laughed as well at his light-heartedness. "We know that Chaldean summoning ritual." He began saying it aloud.

"Oh, you mustn't," I said, clapping my hand over his mouth. "What if it's real?"

"True," he said. "It won't work unless we go to the Laughing Maiden. Oh dear, Iris, you've been too influenced by all that reading and by Old Marsh himself. He is a crackpot. We could no more summon the dead than . . . than we could fly out the windows."

We made jokes about what kind of warriors we would call from the dead to go find our father and make him come home to us. At the Laughing Maiden, Harvey took my hands in his and we recited the words we'd learned from one of my grandfather's books.

Yet, as we suspected, no demon arose, no dead came to do our bidding.

"It's a pity," Harvey said. "If the dead had asked for my first-born, I'd have said yes, for I shan't have any children."

"None at all?"

"None," he said. "Look at our family, Iris. Our grandfather has lost his mind, our father never wishes to be with us. Mother is in her room drinking or taking those cures that cure nothing but drive her further into sleep. Spence is becoming a libertine."

"But you aren't like Spence."

"Aren't I?" he asked, and in his words I realized that there had been something of Harvey's life he had always kept from me, as close as we had been. Perhaps he was different when he was at school. Perhaps he was not the boy I had grown up knowing as my brother. "I am like Spence in some ways. I just don't show it as much as he does. I am private in my Spencerly ways and wiles."

"You're nothing like him."

"If you say so, it's settled then. But really, we are not meant to breed. Only you should have children. You are the good one."

"Why me?"

"Because you understand love," he said, and laid his arm gently across my shoulder. I leaned against him.

We did not return to the house until well after midnight. We sat before the doors of the Tombs beneath the moon and spoke of what life might be like beyond Belerion Hall, what life had been on the island when we were young, and how I would always think of him as Osiris, and he would think of me as Isis.

❧ 5 ❧

I should mention that in the fall, winter, and most of the spring, I was under the thumb of a new and very stern governess named Edyth Bright, who was pretty and young and cruel. When I'd been younger, my governess had been a sweet woman named Miss Alice Ivey, who enjoyed children and the fun that could be had with us. But she accepted a marriage proposal and left us, and "Edyth Blight"—as Harvey called her—entered our lives.

She was as lovely, physically, as the girls in my grandfather's naughty pictures, but she carried a sourness about her that seemed to come directly from having to work among the wealthy. "Not everyone grew up with a room of her own, and if you intend to grow lazy and fat, I will put you out with the sheep," she would scold me when I remained in bed late in the morning, or after the morning's meal. "When I was a girl, I had oat cakes and water for breakfast, and took an ice-cold bath. It is a pity that such luxury is wasted upon someone your age."

During lessons, if I should mistake a noun for a verb, she would slap my hand with a stick until the tears came to my eyes. If I played a tune badly on the piano, she would rap my knuckles. Once, when I sat listening to one of her many lectures on the natural world, she complained that I played with my hair too much. She brought in scissors and told me to cut my hair in those places where my fingers wandered. I could not do this, and began sobbing, begging her forgiveness. She took the scissors back and grabbed the back of my scalp and cut a clutch of long hair. She held it up before my eyes and said, "Now you shan't be so pretty," and repeated this over and over again as if she were somehow broken on the inside.

I felt completely as if I were her prisoner if my brother Harvey wasn't nearby to rescue me. Spence sometimes looked in on my lessons, but without the intention of rescuing me. Spence watched my governess at times, and when she went to her bed at night, he often asked me what kinds of music she liked, or if she had a favorite flower.

Once, when she was prickly with me, I told her that she was a servant of our house and to show respect. She reached for my shoulder and pinched me very hard and leaned over to whisper in my ear, "Someday, you might be where I am and I might be where you are. Someday, I might call *you* 'servant.'"

It wasn't until the winter of my fifteenth year, near the holidays—when I found her with my brother Spence, on the great oriental rug in our grandfather's library—

that I grew to truly hate her. Edyth lay in Spense's arms; her blouse unbuttoned too far; her hair wild like briars; an animal heat in her eyes.

Sprawled on the sofa and floor beside them were the pictures of the nude women. In an instant I realized that the pictures had incited their lusts.

In the next moment, I knew that I finally could destroy Edyth and make her pay for her cruelty to me.

6

I stood in the doorway and said, "Disgusting! Look at you, Edyth *Blight*. You shan't last long in this house now. No one in all of Cornwall will ever employ you again! No one in the entire country! You will be turned out into the street!"

She glanced up at me, her face turning bright red—first with shame, and then with fury. "You little *witch*!" she cried out, while Spence, covering himself up, laughed and rolled to the side as if disinterested in my anger.

I turned away haughtily, for I had won in the battle to rid myself of Edyth. I stomped my way along the corridor, heading straight to the West Wing, where my mother spent her days and nights in bed. Harvey had taken his books to her room that day to study and spend time with her. I would tell them about Edyth and Spence, and how they both needed to be thrown out of the house immediately. I knew that once my mother heard this, she would not let Edyth live under our roof one more day, nor would she hesitate to let others know of Edyth's behavior. And Harvey would help, too. He could scold Spence and send him packing back to university again, and then everything would be good. And perhaps my father would come home to take care of us again.

Edyth raced after me along the hallway, catching up too quickly. She pulled me aside into the alcove beneath a red velvet curtain. I could just see, through the glass of the window, the shape of someone in the garden below.

The gardener's son was out in the sunken garden, plucking at dried branches even while a drizzle of rain came down. I wanted to shout for him to come help me, but I struggled against Edyth's hold.

Out of breath, she warned me, "You cannot understand this. What men and women do. You do not know what you saw." She tightened her grip on my wrists. "I will thrash you, Iris Catherine Villiers. I will thrash you but good. You cannot understand this. You think you do, but you cannot, you little witch."

"I understand *perfectly*," I said, tears in my eyes. "Pretending to be above me. Pretending to have ideals and to talk about great art and literature. Cutting my hair because of vanity. Slapping me whenever the mood takes you. You are sloth and lust and vanity and all the sins combined. *Let me go, I say*." My words had some effect on her, and she loosened her grip slightly. I shook myself free of her and turned toward the window.

I pushed up the latch on the window, thinking that if Percy looked up at me and heard me shout, Edyth might leave me alone for now.

As I moved the latch upward, she pulled me back around, grabbing hold of me again.

"You *swear* you will tell no one," she said as she shook me as if I were a rag doll. "Swear!" She glanced out the window, perhaps seeing Percy there, perhaps wondering what I might be capable of doing.

"I will *not*," I whispered in a snarl, seething as I spoke. "I will tell *everyone*. You will be ruined. You will be *ruined*. You will be out in the street before supper. You're nothing but a . . . a . . ." I quickly tried to think of the worst word I had, but only my grandfather's language came to me. "*Harlot.*"

"Then you will be known as a little liar, missy," Edyth whispered. "Spencer and I will say that you have an unclean mind. I will lock you up with your grandfather. I will . . . I will . . ."

"What? What will you do to me? Kill me? Cut out my tongue? *You're a servant here*," I spat back at her, struggling against her as she held tight.

I leaned toward the open window to cry out to Percy so he would see us and come help me.

Edyth drew back and slapped me as hard as I had ever been slapped in my life.

I felt the back of her hand as it whacked against my cheek.

I fell backward against the window, the freezing pain along my face.

Though this happened in a few seconds, it felt slow and endless, for I cried out in terror as I felt myself going through the opening window, backwards, droplets of rain on my face.

FOUR

Edyth grasped my wrists. Her hands, moistened by sweat, began slipping. She grabbed my waist, but even this was too much for her.

I saw the world upside down, where the gray sky was the earth and the green and brown earth, the sky. Percy Marsh looked up at me from the green sky, though his face was a wash of rain.

Edyth grabbed my legs as I twisted, suspended, out the window.

"Dear God!" she cried out. "Dear God!" She did not mean to let me go, I know that, although I was sure she would, for better I were dead than an eyewitness to her ruination. Yet she groaned and moaned as she held me there and called out for Percy and for Spence and for Harvey and for Mrs. Haworth and for Old Marsh to come help her.

I hung there, looking at this new upside-down world, and thought: *I am going to die. I am going to fall, and my head will hit the flagstones and I will be somewhere else in the next second. I will be wherever you go when you die. Heaven. Hell. The Otherworld. The Other Side. The Upside-Down Land.*

I saw the stone-hedges and remembered what Old Marsh had said, that they had been built from the local stones to keep the dead within their circle. I wondered if I would haunt this place after my fall. If I would stay within the flagstone walk and the cellars and the sunken gardens and the Tombs and the Thunderbox Room and the cliffside of Belerion Hall ever after because of the stone walls that ran along the estate's edges.

"Here? What's all this?" I heard Harvey's voice and the sound of shouts from down the hallway. Then, I heard his voice just above me. "Iris? *Iris?* Don't be afraid, don't be afraid," Harvey said. I felt relief at the sound of his voice. I knew that once he arrived, everything would be all right. I wanted to tell him about the terrible and evil Edyth Blight, and his awful twin Spence, but I was too happy hearing his voice as he came to my rescue.

He and Edyth exchanged some words while I looked down at the flagstones below. *How far was it?* I wondered. *How far a drop?* If I fell, I might only break a leg. Or both legs. Perhaps my head would crack open. Perhaps Percy Marsh would run beneath me and catch me.

Edyth's grip on my legs began slipping again, and I felt a strange freedom as I thought more and more of just dropping.

"It's all right, Iris," Harvey said, his voice soft and comforting. "Don't be afraid. I want you to close your eyes. Will you do that? Close your eyes, and count to ten. Count slowly. By the time you open them, I shall have you here again, up here with me. We will laugh about this. Remember the Great Villiers Trapeze Brother-and-Sister Act? Why, I'll swing you up and over the windowsill and you'll be laughing by the time you open your eyes." His hands were upon my legs, a vise-like grip.

I felt Harvey's strength as he began to slowly draw me up. I heard Spence's voice, too, and for a moment felt other hands on me—both brothers were doing what they could to draw me upward.

Beneath me, Percy and his father had run over, and two of the kitchen girls had run out from the rooms below. One of the girls covered her eyes as if she were looking upward at the sun, which I thought odd given the gray rainy day.

Harvey continued to soothe my fears. "Just think of the Great Villiers Brother-and-Sister Trapeze Act. I'll lift you up. Don't be afraid. It's just like when we were little and I got you up on the swing. Remember? Easy does it. Easy. Yes, close your eyes, yes, close them, Iris. Here were go . . ." He began to sing that little nursery rhyme that our father had taught him and he had taught me on the tree swing in our yard on the island. "Jack, swing *up*, and Jack swing down, *up to the window*, over the ground. Swing over the field and the garden wall—Watch out for Jack Hackaway if you should fall."

I closed my eyes, finally. I felt him drawing me upward toward the window. He slipped a hand under my back. I knew I was nearly back over the window ledge and would soon watch Edyth get her comeuppance.

I stretched my arms up to him, pulling at his forearms as I had as a little girl on the swings, as if I would climb atop his shoulders.

A trapeze act.

He gasped and groaned and shouted a quick curse as if something had caused him to fumble, and his hands slipped.

I reached up again. I wasn't afraid at all, for Harvey was not only half of the Great Villiers Brother-and-Sister Trapeze Act, but he would not fail.

He was a golden boy in a world of brass and tin.

I would learn later that Harvey had leaned so far out the window to draw me upward that he lost his balance and his knee gave out and he tripped over the window ledge.

All I knew, as I opened my eyes in that second, was that he had somehow managed to grab me in an embrace—and we were falling—and it was so fast that it was not like falling to the ground at all, but like sliding along a floor toward a stone wall.

Harvey hugged me close as we fell. I do not remember landing, nor do I remember how solidly he managed to embrace me in that endless fragment of a breath that was our fall, but he would not let me go. I remembered his lavender smell, overwhelming me with sweet scent.

He cushioned me just as a bolt of lightning seemed to flash behind my eyes, and I closed them knowing we had landed on the flagstones.

Something changed inside me during that fall. It was as if a window lifted in my mind, and I could see something I had not noticed a moment earlier. Yet, I did not understand what I saw—what I felt. It was as if a switch had been turned, and a room that had once been darkened became illuminated. I heard a voice whisper to me, *Jack, swing up, and Jack swing down, up to the window, over the ground. Swing over the field and the garden wall—*

I opened my eyes. I felt pain in my back and along my legs and arms, but I was alive. It seemed someone had put a mattress down below, and yet I knew no one had.

Harvey had been my mattress, my cradle.

He lay there, beneath me, holding me tight, his head smashed on the stones and a calm pool of blood beside him, diluted by raindrops.

I finished the rhyme for him, in my head, the voice of a little girl on a swing tied by rope to the thick branch of a tree.

But watch out for Jack Hackaway if you should fall.

Part Two

The Swallow

"Come ye not here to sleep or slumber."

FIVE

Mrs. Haworth had Percy come in and board up the window, for no one wanted to look out from it again. Old Marsh sent me a note that Percy left for me in the hall and Mrs. Haworth brought to my bedside. All he had scribbled down was, "A hasty recovery, miss," signing it "Mr. M."

By February, I could walk again.

In early March, my jaw no longer hurt, and by the following summer only a few noticed my limp. I had such an ache at the core of my being, for a day did not pass that I did not think of Harvey and feel a searing pain at the center of my body as if I were experiencing the throes of death and birth itself.

And still, I walked the hallways and the stairs; I ate now and then, and watched the sea from windows; I sat in the gardens and stared at the flowers and vines as they grew and died and grew, and I wondered why people could not be like this, why if we planted them, they could not grow again.

Edyth remained with us though I ignored any teaching or guidance she offered. No one ever told of what she and Spencer had done; nor did I wish to, though I hated her with all my heart. I blamed her for Harvey's death.

I blamed Spencer for it as well.

I blamed our mother and *Dr. Witherspoon's* tonic and our father and Our Father Who Art in Heaven.

I blamed myself.

I blamed the pictures of the nude women my grandfather had tucked into the old Bible.

~ 3 ~

I had been too weak to attend Harvey's funeral, but they buried him in the Tombs, as many Villiers before him had been buried. I watched from my window as the doors were opened, and the men crouched down to take his coffin through the entryway. I thought of him there, among our ancestors, and wondered how room had been made for his coffin, or how it was sealed, or if they placed it into the stone wall as some had been buried, or into one of the few stone biers left in that passageway of death.

My father returned for two months only, and then left again for his foreign wars. I have no memory of his visit. Lewis came from university but—too much like my father—did not stay long, either. Like my father, my eldest brother was a stranger to me by then, and I barely recognized him.

My mother wept for ages, and when I tried to comfort her, she said, "When they put him in the Tombs, I remembered how scared he was of the trunk. In the play. Do you remember? How he didn't want to go in it, because it scared him to be confined like that in a box. When he was a boy, he didn't like small spaces. I hate thinking of him there."

"He's not there," I whispered as I combed my fingers through her hair. "He's in heaven." I began crying, too, and my mother turned away from me.

"There is no heaven," she said. "It's what people say because they don't want to think about that trunk they will be put in when they die."

My mother, whose health had not returned, remained ill through even the summer season and rarely left her room.

We had become a house of invalids, a house of silences, and a house of sorrow.

❧ 4 ❧

I asked Spence to walk with me to Harvey's grave on a particularly golden day. I still used a cane, and would need his support as we walked the uneven paths through the gardens along the stone walls.

At the doors of the Tombs, I said a few prayers silently. Spence sat down in the grass and offered me his arm to curl up beneath, for his mood had changed. We sat as if we were little children, rather than a girl of sixteen and a man of nearly twenty. We sat the way Harvey and I had often sat down together, out on the grassy summer cliffs.

"Are you all right these days?" he asked.

"Not too much all right," I said.

"I worry for you."

"I worry for all of us," I said.

"I've seen you at night. When you walk up and down the stairs."

"Do I do that?" I asked, not sure I believed him.

He nodded. "At first I thought you might be sleep-walking."

"Perhaps I am."

"Perhaps," he said. "What about this?" He lifted my arm so that my sleeve fell down a bit. There, on my fore-arm, were small marks, as if a cat had clawed me.

"I suppose it will take a while to heal."

He looked me in the eyes as if not believing me.

"My shoulder still hurts, sometimes," I said.

"But these," he tapped my forearm. "These aren't from your fall."

"Yes they are," I said.

We were both silent for several minutes. I had begun wishing intensely that Harvey was with us.

"I miss him so much," Spence said. "You know that, don't you? I miss him so much. He's the first person I ever knew in my life. That sounds absurd, but he was my twin. He's half of me. And he's gone forever. I knew him like I knew myself. We were different. Night and day. If he was good, I would be bad. If he was hard-working, I would be lazy. We had balance. And now, it's gone. There is no balance. I don't know how to be."

"He's still with us," I said, softly.

"I know. I know. In that way that no one ever leaves," and then he turned to me, sobbing as all of us sobbed at times, but mostly in private.

I held my older brother. For a moment, it was like being with Harvey again. I could pretend that his hair was parted on the right. I could pretend the birthmark was behind his ear; I could pretend I smelled lavender rather than that hint of dirt that Spence always had upon his skin.

But I knew there was no birthmark anywhere on Spence's body.

I knew in my heart that Harvey would never hold me like this again.

I knew that Spence's affection was about his vanity. He was not hurt because he missed Harvey. He was hurt because he no longer had a mirror to look at to remind himself of who he might be.

When his heaving sobs had ended, he drew back from me and lay back in the soft grass. "I go back to that day, in my mind," Spence said.

"Please don't," I said.

"I was in the library when I heard the shouts. I went into the hall and saw Harvey running down from the other end, by the doors to mother's room. He stared at me. Perhaps I imagined it. He moved so fast, how could he have stared? But he judged me then. He judged me. Perhaps he knew about Edyth. Perhaps he didn't. He was my twin. We knew about each other, even when we didn't speak of it. Perhaps he forgives me."

"Yes," I said. "He does. I know it."

But I did not mean those words, for I did not forgive Spence, nor did I forgive Edyth. Nor would I allow Harvey to forgive them; for he was the best of our family. I would never forgive myself for my part in this, for if I had only fallen free from Edyth's grasp, Harvey would never have cradled me to his death.

I missed my brother too much to allow his tragedy to be washed away in forgiveness like soapy water down a drain.

When Spence wandered off for a bit, overcome with a need for privacy, I drew up a twig from the ground and wrote in the dirt, in our secret ancient Chaldean magic language, OSIRIS, ISIS SEARCHES FOR YOU.

Beneath this, I drew one of the symbols of Isis herself—an *ankh,* the key of eternal life.

🌿 5 🌿

That night, feeling as if I had been too hard on my older brother for nearly a year, I climbed the stairs to his room. I would knock, and tell him that all was forgiven. That Harvey had blessed us all. That even the sorrow of our lives could be turned into a shining victory over death itself.

But outside his door, I heard her voice in his room.

She was with him.

Edyth.

I listened to their love-talk from the hall. When the lights had gone out in his room, I went to the window where Harvey had held on to me to protect me from death's own embrace.

I peeled back the boards until my fingernails bled.

A shock of cool air burst through from the other side, and I looked out over the sunken garden and across the cliffs to the blackness that was both sea and sky.

I sang softly to the night, "Jack, swing up, and Jack swing down, up to the window, over the ground. Swing over the field and the garden wall—Watch out for Jack Hackaway if you should fall."

~ 6 ~

My rages began then, and I could not contain them.

I found myself in the garden that night, beating my fists against the stone wall until it seemed the rock itself bled. In the cellars the next night, where no one could find me. I stood at the door of the Thunderbox Room and thought of Harvey there, washing up after working in the gardens all day, and out along the cliffs, looking at the locked doors of the Tombs and imagining the bones there, the death, the waste and end of all life.

The world is backwards, I thought.

The living should be dead.

The dead should be living.

The good should be victorious.

The evil should die and stay dead.

I went to the North Wing to hear my grandfather's enfeebled shouts and curses. I nodded my head as he cried out about wrath and redemption and resurrection and smiting the wicked and praising the good.

I understood, then, where his madness had come from: He, too, had experienced the loss of the good and the victory of the evil.

❧ 7 ❧

Sifting through my grandfather's nude photographs in the study, I began to see the women in them as of the devil himself. I went to my grandfather's great mahogany desk and searched for the scissors beneath various old papers.

I neatly cut the heads off the women in the pictures. I imagined each was a state execution, and this would kill the women who had somehow influenced Spence to lie with Edyth. I thought of the two of them passing the filthy pictures back and forth as Spence became aroused with passion and Edyth began to allow him intimacies. I took the scissors and the headless photos into the cellars that day, down into the water closet used by servants that led out into the outdoor stairwell. I decided I would flush the pictures down the drain, out of the house, for—having looked at them—I began to even blame the pictures for that terrible day.

In the Thunderbox Room in the cellars, I looked at the cracked mirror, imagining the demons from my grandfather's books circling around Edyth, tearing at her clothes. I imagined Jezebel and Delilah and Rahab and Ruth and

Naomi, headless, coming toward her with a great pair of scissors and cutting off Edyth's head. I imagined Spence hanging himself from the chandelier in the foyer. All of them dying horribly—even my beloved mother, who had allowed her mind to turn inward and keep her sick so that she would not have to be our mother again; my father, in Burma, or in India, or in one of the war-torn countries that was the source of our wealth; and the Gray Minister, at his own locked window, calling down the Wrath of God upon his household.

My rage burned, and my face felt hot. I leaned over the pump and pushed down on the lever until the ice-cold water poured out into the square sink. I took up a small and worn bar of soap and pressed it to my face. The scent assaulted me. The girls in the kitchen had made this for Harvey. It was my brother's smell. I splashed my face, scrubbing it with soap and then rinsing it off, closing my eyes as the soap stung beneath my eyelids. When I had washed it all off again, I looked at myself in the mirror, but did not see myself.

I saw Edyth's face, and it made me furious to see her.

It was as if she had triumphed in some way with Harvey's death.

It was if his dying had made her permanently part of our family.

As if her words to me when I'd been younger had taken on a reality.

"Someday," she had said, "you might be where I am and I might be where you are."

I wanted her to leave. I wanted her to die. I wanted to expose what she and Spence continued to do in this house. I wanted to destroy them both.

Those nude photographs in my grandfather's Bible were dark and evil, not the beauties of art that I had once imagined them.

No, they were as much demon as the books on summoning demons and ancient spells that my grandfather had collected.

I knew now they were seducers taking from men, from others—to win a battle, to defeat the men that gazed upon them.

They were bad women who sent good men to their deaths.

I took the scissors and looked at my face in the mirror. Looked at Edyth in my mind. At Spence. At my mother.

I hated all of us. Harvey had been too good for the world.

I lifted the scissors and scraped them into the skin of my wrist and carved my brother's secret name into my own flesh.

OSIRIS.

That is when I first heard a slight noise, as if something were scratching at the window. I almost dreaded glancing over, for I was afraid in some childish and irrational way that I had called some demon to my side. The window into the stairwell showed nothing, yet my sense of dread remained.

When I went out through the door, and then through a second doorway into the mossy stone stairwell with its drains that led up to the grounds from the cellars, it was empty.

I returned to the toilet, and the sound began again, as if something had been waiting for me to return.

Now it was more like some small animal—a mouse, perhaps—batting at its confinement. I glanced about the floor, and looked behind the pipes, but saw nothing. The noise continued, and within it I heard the tiniest of chirps, again like a mouse or a small bird; and the thought went through my head that there was a bird trapped in the toilet bowl.

Somehow, I reasoned, briefly, that a bird had flown in, unnoticed, and had gone into the bowl and was drowning. The irrational notion almost made me smile.

I leaned over the crude chamber-pot of a toilet and drew aside the lid. It was full of reddish-brown water. I supposed no one used the water closet that much here. I drew the lid back over the bowl. At the same time, I noticed that the noise had stopped. I laughed. I reasoned too quickly that it had been the pipes themselves making a strange noise, and perhaps just the act of lifting the toilet lid had been enough to end it.

But the effect of this was as if I had opened an unseen door, or unlatched another hidden shelf in my grandfather's library. I felt a strange coldness clutch at my throat, and the hairs at the back of my neck stood up as goose bumps covered my arms.

The strange scratching and chirping sound began again.

This time, I was sure it came from the bowl beneath the lid.

≫ 8 ≪

I stared at the bowl as the sound became louder, as if—yes—a bird fluttered its wings as it drowned in that dirty water.

I drew the lid aside.

In the water, a swallow—the kind I often saw at twilight swooping and flying along the trees and the eaves of our home—batted at the water as if trying to fly upward.

I felt, for the first time, as if I stood at the edge of some borderland, ill-defined by the physical world.

I thought that, like my grandfather, I might be going mad.

The bird drowned as soon as I reached for it. When I took it out into the night to lay its body down upon the flagstones, I was convinced that I had begun losing my grasp of what was real and what was not.

But I felt that brief spark of what I would later come to regard as psychic ability. That window—which opened in my mind when I fell with my brother—seemed to burst wide again.

❧ 9 ❧

That night, I stayed up until dawn, poring over my grandfather's books of the sacred and the profane.

At sunrise, I went to Spence's room.

I opened the door to look in on the two of them lying in bed.

I could not even look directly at Edyth or my brother, but instead looked through them.

Edyth shrieked when she saw the scissors in my hands, and while I tried to explain that it was not to hurt her or him, Spence leapt from his bed and knocked them from my fingers.

The scissors scuttled across the floor toward the wardrobe.

"You have to let this go!" he shouted. "You are driving all of us mad! You had no right to come into my room! You have no right to interfere with Edyth! It was you who killed him, Iris! You with your foolishness! I was there when you fell! I stood behind Harvey when he reached for you. You pulled him out of that window, Iris! We could have saved both of you, but you *pulled him out*!"

"It's a lie! It's a lie!" I cried, covering my face, trying to block out his terrible voice.

"Ask anyone who was there!" he shouted, his face above me, a monstrous face, a liar's face. "Ask Edyth! No, ask Percy! Ask Elizabeth from the kitchen! They all saw it. They all saw you reach up and pull him down! If you had just let him draw you up, you both would be here. You are the one who took him to his death! I could kill you, Iris! *I could kill you*!"

SIX

I ran out to the Tombs with keys in hand, stumbling several times. My own tears blinded me. I did not understand why my brother had told me such terrible lies, but I knew he was wrong.

I did not pull Harvey out the window. I could not have done it. We were doing our old trapeze act, and I was meant to reach for him. Yet, in my mind, as I recalled those brief moments before we fell, I could not help but now see that Spence was correct. I had been too eager and had felt Harvey lose his balance as I reached up for his arms. But I did not pull him out of the window. He had fallen; it was an accident. If anyone was to blame, it was Edyth Blight. Edyth Blight and her harlotry, and slapping me hard enough that I fell backward from the tall window.

Edyth had killed him and had nearly killed me.

I pressed my hands to my face as I fell down in the grass in front of the doors of the Tombs. *Please, Harvey, let me know you forgive me. Please.*

I unlocked the doors of the Tombs and ducked my head to take the steps down among the narrow rock corridors where the Villiers were buried.

I checked the graves marked along the plastered stone wall and looked in the recesses of rock where stone biers had been placed.

I found Harvey's tomb, and tore a strip of cloth from my dress. I used it as a blindfold, for I wanted to block out all of the world around me. I used it the way Old Marsh had told me blindman's buff had once been played, not as a game, but as a way of speaking with the dead. I turned about until I was disoriented. Strangely, I did feel as if I had stepped into another world, and in that self-imposed darkness, I began to feel as if others were there, surrounding me.

I wanted to see Harvey again. I wished with all my might that he would come to me.

I prayed first to God, and then to the gods I had heard once roamed this land.

I nearly conjured his face in my mind.

Remembering how we had once tried to summon our father by using an old spell, I recited this as well. I imagined that I held the bones of the dead in my arms as I said this, and wished for them to rise up from their pathways and bring my brother back to me, to life.

"Let's summon the dead," Harvey had said to me our first spring in Belerion Hall. He and I had laughed as we sat down at the Laughing Maiden after supper and said that we wanted to see our father. Harvey used a handkerchief for a blindfold and put it on, turning around and around a few times. At first we laughed more, and then we grew sad, for our father was alive. We could not summon the living with the ancient Chaldean summoning spell, and it was the living we wanted then.

When the night had grown dark, Harvey had slipped his arms around me in an embrace that was both comfortable and familiar and that still haunted me after a few years had gone by.

We had talked of death then, and of life, and of how we would both grow up and move away from Belerion Hall. "But I will always find you," he said. "Just summon me from the ends of the earth. Just call me here."

The smell of lavender; the whisper at my ear as he told me how much I meant to him and always had; and how he called me Isis after our play, and I called him Osiris. And like Isis, I told him, I would always find him and bring him back home with me.

That night had seemed innocent and sweet, but as I stood before his grave with a blindfold on so that I might be distracted from my purpose, I felt a shiver of terror go through me.

Yet, I could not stop.

I prayed to the dead.

Send him to me.

No matter how.

Bring my brother home to me.

I will give you anything for him to return. Anything at all. My life. My life. All lives. All that I can.

Hours passed, and I heard a few sounds, as if some small animal—a rat, perhaps—skittered along the carved rock floor.

Then, I heard what seemed to be a man clearing his throat. Yet I did not take off my blindfold to see who was there with me. I did not want to break the spell of imagining that Harvey had arisen as if he were Christ

from the tomb. I knew that once I drew that blindfold from my eyes, I would see the nothing that was there: the carved rock with the old tombs and burial places. While the blindfold remained, I could believe that he stood beside me, nearly touching me.

I could believe that I smelled lavender.

As I was about to give up this foolishness, I felt a draft of chilly air as if a window had opened, but within me. Some call this the higher self, but for me, it felt as if it was someone other than me, some other girl. I called her Isis, in order to see her as different from myself.

Come back to me, Harvey. Come now. Come from those highways of the dead. I cannot live without you. I cannot live if I can't see you again.

❧ 2 ❧

Later that night, I stood looking out the window, remembering Harvey's embrace as we fell from it.

The moon's white light cast itself upon the sunken garden just beyond the flagstone walk. The wind blew in gusts from the sea and lightning played along the far reaches of the horizon, though it would be hours before the storm came to our estate.

I saw a wriggling movement in the shadows of the stone walls.

A whirl of motion, as of leaves and seedlings stirred up by a sudden breeze.

As if I were connecting parts of a puzzle drawn upon the air, I saw a strange form manifesting itself from the soft white milk thistles that blew in a circular motion at the garden wall.

It seemed the outline of a man.

He arrived in a breeze where thistle and deer-broom whirled and formed a pattern that at first I could not distinguish as anything other than a flurry of wisps and seedlings. But gradually, as the wind rose up, the flurry grew to a small whirlwind in one corner of the garden, clearly visible to me.

Within it, I saw a man's face and form, and though it did not seem to be Harvey, I felt it was. I felt I had summoned him and conjured him and had stepped into a kind of happy madness, half-believing he had returned and half-knowing I had let my imagination run away with me.

I went down to the garden, hoping to see him. My heart beat as if it wanted to burst from my body; my

throat grew dry as I ran along the walls to the gate into the sunken gardens.

When I reached the place where the milk thistle had blown, I saw nothing but the tiny seedlings whirling in the brisk wind.

This did not dampen my belief.

I walked toward the Tombs, following the thin paths between the stone-hedges to get to the cliff.

❧ 3 ❧

The doors were thrown back as if by a great force of wind, and a man stood there with a lantern.

He glanced over at me, shining his lantern my way.

Old Marsh wore a look of sorrow upon his face. "You called him, miss. You called him. You must send him back now. You must send him back. He won't be the brother you remember. It ain't his spirit comes back. I told you that. It's the soul of death comes back, that's what it is, miss. The soul of death in disguise like your brother. Only the one who called him can send him back. I saw the bird in the cellars, in the bowl, miss. I know what you done. I know what you called."

❧ 4 ❧

I was still but a girl, and even at that, my world had been one of shelter and privilege. I had no real understanding of life or death, and when the gardener told me about what he had seen in the Thunderbox Room, I laughed. "It's him. It's all him!" I said.

"Miss, it's you. You been touched—the fall did it. The fall almost took you with the dead. But you come back and you got that touch of something. I seen it before with a woman in the village. She near-drowned and when she come back, she got touched, too."

"If it's me, then I'm glad," I said. "I want him back. I want him back with us."

"Unseen things come with accidents," Old Marsh mumbled to himself, clucking like a roosting hen. "Happens sometimes. I heard a man got hit with an iron bar once and he predicted the future. You, miss, you opened a door to the dead when you fell. That's what it is. And you keep opening it. Need to close it now."

"But if Harvey's here," I said, "I just want to see him. Just once more. Just once."

"I told you," he said. "I warned you. It ain't him. It's like something that knows what you want and shows it to you. But it's only reflecting what you want to see."

"What's there to be afraid of?" I said. "Thistles floating in a breeze? A swallow drowning in a bowl?"

"You shall know soon enough, miss," he said, sadness in his voice. "For it doesn't stop until it's good and ready to stop. Or until the one who calls up the dead, sends them back. He will ask you to promise him something now. And you must make that promise so that he will go back into death's embrace. When the dead been promised, the dead be paid."

❦ 5 ❦

As we stood there, I saw a shadow figure walking out along the stone-hedges, nearest the cliff. "He's there! Look!" I shouted, my heart beating fast.

"Miss! Miss!" Old Marsh cried out, and when he looked at the cliff side, he dropped his lantern to the earth and I heard a terrible coughing coming from the old gardener.

I knew it was Harvey, and I ran toward the figure, but as I reached him, no one was there at all. And yet, right up until I reached the spot where he had stood, I saw Harvey's features more clearly in that dark night than I had on any bright afternoon when he had been alive.

I glanced around, my arms outstretched as if I were truly playing blindman's buff with him where sight itself was my blindfold.

"Come back! I'm here!" I cried. "Come back! Show me! Show me!"

I sobbed and cried out to God and the angels and the devils and all the gods that had once been in Cornwall. Tears began to cloud my vision and my thoughts. I began whirling around and around, hoping to see Harvey again.

Hoping to call him from my mind, from his grave, into a physical form again as I had seen him a shadow and a whirlwind of thistle.

I heard Old Marsh's calls at a distance but ignored his warnings. He shouted for me to draw back from the edge, his voice nearing as I spun about.

I turned around and around, feeling as if I were dancing, as if Harvey would stop me from whirling. I knew in some reckless way that I spun in this slow, graceful dervish dance toward the cliff's edge, but I no longer cared. *Let me fall*, I thought. *Let me fall so I can be with him. Fall the way I was meant to fall down from the window. I belong at the bottom of the sea, on the rocks, in the harbor. I belong to Death. I belong to Harvey. I owe him my life.*

And just as I felt my foot catch in a crag of a rock and a dirt hole, and looked down to see the crashing sea below, and know that I might fall and all of this would be over and that I would join him in the Tombs and follow those paths of the dead, someone grabbed me about the waist and drew me to the grass again. I fell backwards onto Old Marsh, and he fell, as well, so that I lay atop him. "Marsh," I said, "Marsh, Marsh." I wept and laughed and tried to rise up, but he pulled back against him and I felt a strange strength in the old man's arms.

"You called me back," Harvey whispered in my ear.

SEVEN

❦ 1 ❦

My brother, in flesh and bone, had returned from the dead and had drawn me back from death itself and wrapped me in his embrace.

I felt as if I were freezing as he held me.

❦ 2 ❦

I struggled against him, but he held me so tightly that I began to find it difficult to breathe.

The lavender of his whisper chilled me. "You should not have ignored Old Marsh, Iris." Although my brother's voice spoke, and the small hairs at the back of my neck rose up against his warm breath, it was not Harvey, and yet it was. He spoke in a way that seemed almost foreign, and yet I knew it was my brother—the smell of him, the feel of his arms, and even a strange perverse comfort came to me as he held me there in the grass. His voice sounded as if he were just learning to form consonants and vowels. Gradually as he spoke, his voice was his again, and I almost felt comforted by it. "I am sorry to tell you, my sister, but there is a price when you call the dead back. It will be paid. It is your debt. Do you remember the story of the boy and the warriors? The debts of those who call the dead will be paid."

I felt as if ice ran in my veins as he spoke; this man that was not Harvey and yet was wholly him.

As he clutched me, I craned my neck that I might see Old Marsh and call to him to rescue me, but Harvey whispered, "He came to the cliff's edge to draw you back, but when he saw me, my sweet, I'm afraid his weary heart gave out. Poor old chap. His eyes went wide and the pipe dropped from his lips and spittle ran down his white beard. But then, you did promise in your prayers to the dead that you would give anything for me to come back to you, didn't you?"

❦ 3 ❦

After a brief interval, my dead brother released me. I lay on my side, wondering if my sanity had fled me, or if this were true.

If I had truly resurrected him from death.

In the flesh.

I lay with him out in the wet grass, near the fallen body of our gardener not more than twenty feet away from us.

This is me, I thought. *I have a talent. I call the dead back. I am like that boy of the legends. I am like the Maiden of Sorrow.*

I thought of that small bird in the bowl of the Thunderbox Room. The bird that had materialized, as if my mind had created it again and again. As if something had broken in my mind when my rage had grown too unwieldy, so that I could not quite turn off this ability.

I sat up, finally, looking at him.

Harvey, wearing the clothes he'd been buried in, sat with his legs crossed. He had picked up a small blossom in his hand, and marveled at it.

"Did you miss life?" I asked.

He closed his eyes for a moment, and when he opened them again, I sensed a seething anger, yet his voice seemed calm and steady.

"You must pay for all this. I had gone to a beautiful place. To a place that makes this earth seem ugly and monstrous. All I see here is terror and madness, my sister."

I looked out across the expanse of night, the moon an opal above the sea. I wanted him to stop. "You're here now. You're home. You're with me," I said.

He leaned closer, his breath upon my ear, and spoke in whispers. "I was in paradise, and with me were creatures more radiant than any of this world. The trees that blossomed there were full of the spirits of the eternal. The air was inspiration itself. The grasses sang music that was finer than any you have known. All that was lost to the world was found there. All to which I had felt empty in this life, filled. All that had been mystery, answered. All of my ignorance was cured with the lamp of illumination, raised by a maiden of knowledge."

He drew back from me and covered his face with his hands. Was he weeping? It seemed so, yet in his remembering of death, I felt as if he were describing the greatest of joys. "It is more magnificent than what I thought heaven might be, and yet it is all of its wonder, as well." He wiped his eyes and reached out for me. I felt the warmth of life in his flesh as he clasped my hand. "Iris, we are shut off from it in this life because if any knew its magnificence, life itself would end, for all who are living would seek death. But as the egg must be in the nest for the bird to fly from it, so the living must live and die when nature intends so that the shell may be broken at the point when the living have wings to fly. It is as if in life we are blind, and in death we see. In life we think in error, but in death we know and love and understand. Those who died many centuries before me told their stories, and of the journey we might take in this new existence, and the questions we might ask of the great kings of this new world. I fell in love there, and she loved me."

"But you were dead. You were gone," I protested, tears filling my eyes. "My life was at an end without you."

He laughed as if at a great joke. "Death is not the end of things, my sister. It is the beginning of a greater adventure than this small life you cherish can hold. And beyond these shores of death, there are great ships that fly from the golden seas to the skies of pearl. I heard of wonders from those travelers who had been dead many thousands of years. These lie beyond death itself, in another place where the dead may journey. And you," he said, sadness in his face and the slump of his shoulders. "You call me from that. From the arms of my beloved. From the tales of all worlds past. From the eternal blessedness. Called me with those ancient curses and that window."

"Window?" I asked.

"You know of it," he said.

He stepped closer to me and pressed his thumb to the center of my forehead. His touch was warm as any living man's might be. "Here." He dropped his hand to his side and looked at me with an intense scrutiny. In the legends of the dead returning, it was often said that their eyes were empty or pitch black, but his eyes were the warm blue eyes of my brother. His hair was dark and had grown long in death, and his skin, though pallid, glowed with life. "In your mind. The moment I died. I felt it, too. A window opened inside you. A window, and you are on its ledge. It is why you could call me at all. But I wish . . . I wish you had not."

He walked slowly with an uncertain gait over toward the Laughing Maiden stone. I got up to follow him, and as we reached it, he pointed at the grass.

Old Marsh lay there, his eyes wide and his mouth open, his tongue hanging out. "Fear stopped his heart. Death came with me and touched him. Look, he is like a shell," Harvey said. "Do you see? We are shells, and inside us, the bird is born that must fly. Poor old man. I loved him, and I loved his stories. It was not meant to be his time."

Harvey bent down and pressed the dead man's tongue back between his lips, closing his mouth. Then, he put his fingers over his eyes, shutting them. "The body at death is at rest. At peace. Do you see this? No, no, you see the terror of death. I tell you, Iris, there is more terror in a day of life than there is at the moment of death. It is as if a door has opened to a prison, though you do not believe it is a prison while you exist within it." He turned to look back at me. "Do you know what I felt when I died?"

I shook my head, more tears coming to my eyes. "Please don't speak of it, Harvey. Please. I can't bear to remember. You are alive now. You are here. That is all that matters."

"I felt as if I could truly breathe," he said. He whispered a prayer over Old Marsh's body. "He is, right now, seeing the green cliffs at the other side. The mermaids along the shore sing to him. The light—it is like all lights, and yet like none I had ever before seen. Perhaps his wife is there to greet him. Or an old love. Sometimes, they wait. Sometimes, you see the dead come in to the harbor, and their old dogs are all along the docks, wagging their tails, for they have waited for their masters and mistresses for many years. You see mothers who have missed their sons. Fathers who had never spoken of love to their children, ready to embrace them as they voyage from the end of life. It shows the lies of this world, you see. We are wrong about so many things here. Mankind has done terrible things, yet we are forgiven. Those who have been trodden upon are lifted up there. All wrong is righted." He wiped at the edge of his eyes though he shed no tears. "You do not know what you have done, Iris. You do not know."

"But I love you," I whispered feebly. "I missed you. I could not bear it, knowing I might have . . . that I . . . that if I had fallen . . ."

"Shh," he said, rising up again. He put his hand over my mouth. His hand felt warm, full of blood, the hand of a living man. "Death is a gift, so long as it is nature's hand. But this," he drew his hand away, and nodded toward the dead man in the grass. "When we are called back unnaturally, Death demands a price, for there is always a balance. If I am alive, then someone else must die before his time. This is what you have done. But he is the lucky one. He is at peace. I know what awaits him, and I envy him."

"You are truly yourself," I said, surprised even as I said it. "I feared you might be . . ."

"The soul of Death?" he asked, with a weary grin upon his face. "You call it 'death' to smudge filth upon it. You should call it 'the infinite.' That is what it is. It is existence without end. It is world without end, amen."

I could not help myself. I nearly threw myself at him, embracing him as he had embraced me when he drew me back from the cliff. I wept against his collar. "Please forgive me, Harvey. But I could not live without you. I could not let you leave. It is not home if you are not here."

"So be it," he whispered against my ear. "But we will both pay a price for what you have done, I am afraid."

He would not return with me to the house, but insisted on going to the Tombs. "I am more comfortable there," he said. "The bones of the dead remind me of that wonderful place I've left."

～ 4 ～

So, he slept his first night in his grave, and swore me to secrecy that I not tell Spence or our mother or any of the household of his return.

At dawn, I went to find Percy Marsh to tell him that his father had died. The household was in a flurry over this, and my brother Spence went off to arrange a funeral for the loyal groundskeeper who had served Belerion Hall for more than forty years.

By late afternoon, I went to the Tombs again to look at my brother as he slept, for the dead sleep in the day and rise at sunset.

When he opened his eyes at dusk, my brother begged me to kill him. "I have dreamed of it again. I long to go there," he said.

But I could not bring myself to hurt him. At night, we walked along the cliff's edge and he told me much of what he could remember of the land of the dead, although he had already begun forgetting parts of it. He asked me if I had seen other manifestations of my talent—had the bird come back? What of the whirling of the thistles? Had I seen anything in the sunken gardens? When I told him that none of these things—or any others—had occurred again, he grew silent. I asked him why this was important to him, for I felt these were outward signs of the grace bestowed upon me for raising him from his tomb. He would not tell me, although he spoke of "debt of return" and the "balance of dissonance."

On the third night, when he rose from the Tombs, he told me that Death itself spoke to him in a dream. "Do you remember the play? Of Osiris in Egypt? Do you know why Isis sought Osiris and brought him back from the dead?"

"Because he was her brother," I said. "And because she loved him dearly."

"No," Harvey said, turning away from me to face the sea beneath the cliffs. "It was because she was jealous that Death had him when she wanted him all for herself. Many died so that Isis could bring Osiris back from the land of the dead."

Briefly, he looked back at me and in the moonlight, perhaps he smiled. "Do you know something else? Life has made me afraid of death again. That is what it is meant to do. Look down there." He motioned for me to come close to him. He pointed down to the darkness below the cliffs, the sound of the crashing waves; the moon, as it emerged from behind a cloud, cast an eerie light upon the rocks far below us. "To fall from a window is terrifying. But to fall to the rocks, to the sea, is a poem."

I tried to draw him back from the cliff's edge, but he pushed me away, and I fell onto the grass.

My dead brother stepped off the edge of the world and went to his death again.

EIGHT

❧ 1 ❧

When the body was found, swept up by the sea not a mile away, it was not known who it was, but upon examination, the local doctor, who acted often as not as coroner, claimed that the man had been dead for at least a year or more, judging by the rotting of the corpse.

❧ 2 ❧

I slept for the next several nights better than I had in many months. Harvey was at peace, and the terrible mistake I had made had been fixed, though I was heartbroken by losing him a second time.

Spence and Edyth announced their engagement, and I did not begrudge them their happiness. Our mother finally told us that our father had long ago left her for a woman in India and would probably never return again to his own ancestral home or to his wife and children.

And though I felt terrible sadness at the loss of my brother again, I remembered his stories of this place of death and of new life—this place of the infinite, the radiance, the magnificence. I grew happy thinking of him there, not as Osiris who needed resurrection, but as a man whom I had once loved as my brother named Harvey Villiers who had gone on to a finer place, a place where I might someday see him at the docks when my own ship of death brought me to the harbor.

But one twilight, when I walked with Percy Marsh through the gardens, I saw a figure out at the Tombs—a man who seemed to be crouched down and nearly crawling on his belly.

When Percy left to return to his cottage, I went out in the hazy light as the evening darkened.

Harvey lay there on the ground, his wounds unhealed, his face torn and bloodied. He had dug his way out of the earth—this was evident from the filth upon him.

He said nothing, for his tongue had been eaten away by fish and his teeth had been broken to nubs in the fall. Half of his scalp had been peeled back and was rotting.

But I understood, and I went with him along the path.

I sat with him in the doorway of the Tombs and re-membered our childhood, and the swings and the win-dow and the play of Isis and Osiris and the trunk he had been afraid to climb into one day when he was too old to be afraid of such things.

In my mind, he whispered, *Death would not take me again. I cannot heal. I am neither living nor dead.*

"I'm sorry for what I did," I said.

Old Marsh went in my place. There is no room for me among the dead.

"Forever?" I asked.

He did not answer. I suppose he did not know. He seemed more like the little boy I had known when I was young—in our happiest times on the island, riding a tree swing, playing games near the water's edge—than the corpse of a young man. He hugged me as a child might, and made sounds as if he were weeping.

At dawn, when he went to sleep in the Tombs, I dried all my tears as I helped him crawl into the coffin, with those dark sockets where his eyes had once rested staring up at me.

I drew the lid over his coffin and nailed it in place, and then sealed it again.

I slept several nights near him, and heard his tapping at the coffin. At first it was rapid. He moaned in pain. He made shrieking noises as if he were terrified of being trapped within that box.

I bit my lip to remain silent. I held my hands together as if in prayer to keep from wanting to open his coffin again.

I cried as he knocked against it, kicking at it from within, making guttural noises that must have been cries of torment.

You are Osiris, I thought. *Trapped in your sarcophagus. I am Isis. But I will not release you. You have to die. If you can die, you will do so here. Please forgive me.*

Gradually, after several nights, he stopped making any noise at all.

≫ 3 ≪

He did not speak in my mind, though I wished he would.

I did not open his tomb again, and when my mother died the following year, I took my inheritance and traveled overseas because I did not want to be near my brother's tomb.

Some nights—whether in Paris or Cairo or New York—when I felt that window in my mind open, I thought I heard my brother Harvey's voice. I could never understand what he was saying, for it was all whispering and strange utterances.

I hope that death has finally taken him, but even as I write this, he may be in that tomb, still, my beloved wonderful brother, buried alive but without the release of death, hunger without satisfaction, thirst without end, terror until the world itself might end.

Old Marsh had told us that the trick of calling the dead back to life was a one-way street, for no one in all of history had ever learned the way to send the dead back to Death again.

But the stone-hedges of the Tombs keep him in, and though my brother Spence and his wife Edyth now own Belerion Hall, I wonder if someone—someday—will hear him tap at the edge of his tomb.

I wonder if someone will break open that coffin and see what has become of my brother Harvey.

Will he be there with flesh and bones? Will he be dust, moving eternally, within a stone bier? Or will Death take pity on him, and on me? Will Death call

him back, across the shores to that radiant journey? Or will he forever be there, trapped in a box until the world itself comes to an end?

I loved him more than life itself. I had called him back to life from that open window inside myself—that place where I could speak with the dead themselves, if I loved them enough.

I know the secret that Isis herself knew when she resurrected her brother Osiris, and the secret that the Maiden of Sorrow knew when she brought her lover back from the dead, and which the boy knew after he had grown up and owed his first-born to the dead warriors. Old Marsh himself knew.

The secret is:

Death has a price, and all who bargain with the dead must pay it.